RUSSIAN OPTIMISM:
DARK NURSERY RHYMES TO CHEER YOU RIGHT UP

EDITED AND TRANSLATED BY BEN ROSENFELD
ILLUSTRATED BY DOV SMILEY

ISBN: 978-0-9908552-0-0

Design by Chris James

BigBenComedy
New York, NY
www.BigBenComedy.com

DEDICATIONS

This book is dedicated to the following people who made this project possible:

Alex Rosenfeld and Marina Aparina: For Inspiring This Project

Chris Antzoulis: For Connecting Ben and Dov
Alyssa Wolff: For Publishing Guidance

Cory Doctorow and BoingBoing.net
Tyler Cowen and MarginalRevolution.com
Tyler Gildin, Connor Toole and EliteDaily.com

Joshua Alan Simon and Alicia Blair Caldwell Simon
Josh Sacks

Anastasia Saltarelli
Paul Miller
Katrina Mills
Scott Lurowist

Michael Quaintance
Katy Costello
Patrick Bittner
Mikhail Krylov: Don't stop composing
Nicholas Thaw in honor of Tatiana Gapkovskaya
Theora Cheatham
Stefan Hofer
Catherine G. Donahue
Aleksandr Y. Troyb
Xavier "Харитон" IrAal
Douglas Candano / Дуглас Кандано
Ali Farahnakian and The People's Improv Theater

TABLE OF CONTENTS

INTRODUCTION

Last year, I was in a funk and visited my dad. To cheer me up, he started reading some dark Russian nursery rhymes. The stories were so morbid and over the top that I laughed and laughed. I realized my life wasn't that bad and the joy came back. Shortly thereafter, I decided to share these gruesomely funny rhymes with the English-speaking world.

I was born in the Soviet Union and my family immigrated to the United States when I was a child. Speaking Russian at home while living in America gave me a unique perspective of the similarities and differences between Russia and America.

The biggest cultural difference is the level of optimism. Generally speaking, Americans expect each generation to accomplish more than the previous one. Russians expect each generation to suffer and be miserable. In reality, we all suffer the same, but Americans view suffering as a temporary setback whereas Russians see it as inevitable.

This cultural difference is also reflected in movies. Russian films don't usually have happy endings, and many Russians look down on mainstream American movies because of all the predictable happy endings. In an American film, no matter how much trouble the protagonist is in, he always prevails. Russian movies aren't usually as predictable. If it looks like the main character might not make it, he probably won't.

When I came across these dark Russian nursery rhymes, I thought they truly captured the difference between cultures. These poems are a dark way of saying, "Don't be so sad, things could be worse."

All of these short tales have an A-A, B-B or A-B, A-B rhyme scheme. As an editorial decision, I decided to not rhyme them in English. Instead, the translation focuses on conveying the meaning. In the following pages, I've shared the original Russian rhyme, the English translation and transliteration.

I hope you'll be able to recite your favorite rhymes in Russian and surprise the Russian speakers in your life with something more entertaining than a simple "da," "nyet" or "privet." So go ahead and use this Russian Optimism to cheer up someone in your life.

- Ben Rosenfeld, New York City, November 2014

1

RUSSIAN OPTIMISM

THE BRIGHT SIDE

In my childhood, my mom gouged out my eyes,
So that I wouldn't find the jam.
Now I don't watch movies and I don't read fairy tales,
But on the bright side, I smell and hear really well.

Мне мама в детстве выколола глазки,
Чтоб я в шкафу варенье не нашёл.
Теперь я не хожу в кино и не читаю сказки,
Зато я нюхаю и слышу хорошо.

Mne mama v detstve vykolola glazki,
Chtob ia v shkafu varen'e ne nashel.
Teper' ia ne khozhu v kino i ne chitaiu skazki,
Zato ia niukhaiu i slyshu khorosho.

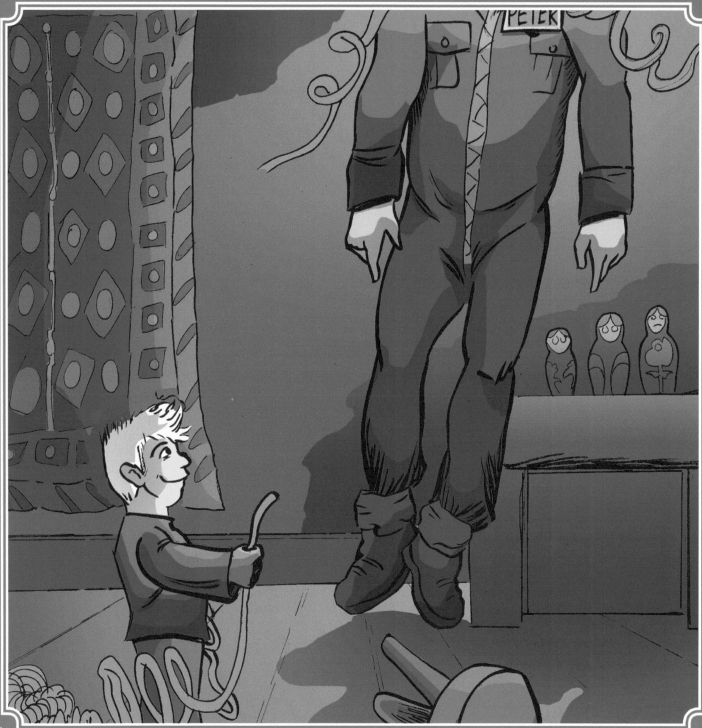

RUSSIAN OPTIMISM

DON'T ASK STUPID QUESTIONS

I asked Peter the electrician,
"Why is there copper wire around your neck?"
He didn't respond,
His boots just swayed quietly.

Я спросил электрика Петрова,
"Почему у Вас на шее медный провод?"
Ничего в ответ он не сказал,
Только тихо ботами качал.

Ia sprosil elektrika Petrova,
"Pochemu u Vas na shee mednyi provod?"
Nichego v otvet on ne skazal,
Tol'ko tikho botami kachal.

RUSSIAN OPTIMISM

DIGGING A HOLE

A little boy was digging a hole in the ground.
Suddenly his shovel hit metal.
His arms are on the pine tree, his balls on the oak tree:
You should be more careful playing with landmines.

Маленький мальчик ямку копал.
Вдруг по железу ударил металл.
Руки - на елке, яйца - у дуба:
С миной нельзя обращаться так грубо.

Malen'kii mal'chik iamku kopal.
Vdrug po zhelezu udaril metall.
Ruki - na elke, iaitsa - u duba:
S minoi nel'zia obrashchat'sia tak grubo.

RUSSIAN OPTIMISM

MOM'S BEDROOM

From mom's bedroom,
A crooked legged cripple
Emerged. It was dad... I walk the same way!
Our gene pool is bad.

Как из маминой из спальни,
Кривоногий и хромой
Вышел папа... Я такой же!
Генофонд у нас плохой.

Kak iz maminoi iz spal'ni,
Krivonogii i khromoi
Yyshel papa... Ia takoi zhe!
Genofond u nas plokhoi.

RUSSIAN OPTIMISM

THE OLD LAWNMOWER

An old man was cutting the lawn,
His blade caught a pair of lovers.
The red blood covered the grass,
Don't fuck in the morning.

Дедушка в поле травку косил,
Пару влюбленных косой зацепил.
Красною кровью покрылась трава,
Не занимайтесь любовью с утра!

Dedushka v pole travku kosil,
Paru vliublennykh kosoi zatsepil.
Krasnoiu krov'iu pokrylas' trava,
Ne zanimaites' liubov'iu s utra!

MOM'S GIFTS

Mom gave her kids some gifts:
Peter got an axe. Sergey got a metal pick.
Misha got a crow bar. Vasya got a knife...
Their drunk neighbor doesn't bother them anymore.

Мама детишкам своим подарила:
Пете - топорик, Сереженьке - шило,
Митеньке - ломик, а Васеньке - ножик...
Пьяный сосед больше их не тревожит.

Mama detishkam svoim podarila:
Pete - toporik, Serezhen'ke - shilo,
Miten'ke - lomik, a Vasen'ke - nozhik...
P'ianyi sosed bol'she ikh ne trevozhit.

RUSSIAN OPTIMISM

THE HOUSE GUESTS

A little girl asked her mom for a candy.
Her mom said, "Put your fingers in the electrical socket!"
Her dress burnt up, her bones charred,
For a long time, the houseguests laughed at this prank.

Дочка у мамы просила конфетку.
Мама сказала: - Сунь пальцы в розетку!
Платье сгорело, обуглились кости,
Долго над шуткой смеялись все гости.

Dochka u mamy prosila konfetku.
Mama skazala: - Sun' pal'tsy v rozetku!
Plat'e sgorelo, obuglilis' kosti,
Dolgo nad shutkoi smeialis' vse gosti.

THE HARMONICA

A little girl found a razor in the bathroom.
"What is this?" She asked her dad.
Her dad replied: "It's a lip harmonica."
Her smile got wider and wider.

Девочка в ванной бритву нашла.
"Что это?" - папу спросила она.
Папа ответил: "Губная гармошка."
Все шире и шире улыбка у крошки.

Devochka v vannoi britvu nashla.
"Chto eto?"- papu sprosila ona.
Papa otvetil: "Gubnaia garmoshka."
Vse shire i shire ulybka u kroshki.

RUSSIAN OPTIMISM

SCHOOL'S OUT

A mom whipped her son because he got a D.
At night, he went to the fireplace and took the poker.
Now he doesn't have to study for a whole year:
Mom is stuck in the hospital for a long time.

Мама за двойку отшлепала сына.
Ночью он взял кочергу из камина.
Можно теперь целый год не учиться:
Мама надолго застряла в больнице.

Mama za dvoiku otshlepala syna.
Noch'iu on vzial kochergu iz kamina.
Mozhno teper' tselyi god ne uchit'sia:
Mama nadolgo zastriala v bol'nitse.

RUSSIAN OPTIMISM

CHERRIES

The kids stole some cherries from a yard.
Grandma Vera was very happy:
Thankfully she'd coated the trees with poison,
The village will have a lot of memorial services.

Дети украли вишни из сада.
Бабушка Вера была очень рада:
Не зря она сбрызнула ядом деревья,
Много поминок будет в деревне !

Deti ukrali vishni iz sada.
Babushka Vera byla ochen' rada:
Ne zria ona sbrysnula iadom derev'ia,
Mnogo pominok budet v derevne!

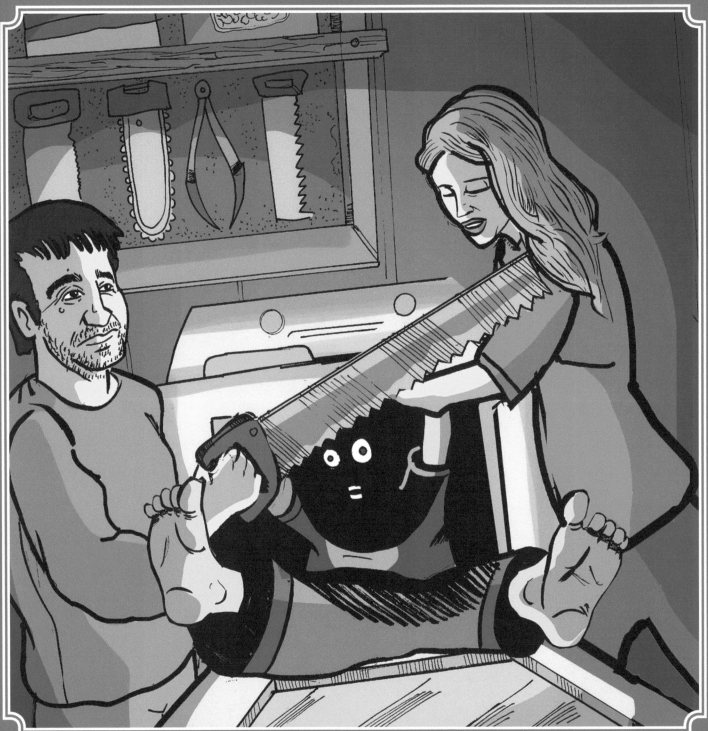

RUSSIAN OPTIMISM

DINNER

Mom looked at Volodya with sorrow:
No, he won't fit into the stove!
His dad went to the closet looking for the saw,
They really need to serve roasted meat at dinner.

Мама с тоскою смотрит на Вовку:
Нет, не войдет целиком он в духовку!
Папа в кладовке ищет пилу,
Очень нужна буженина к столу.

Mama s toskoyu smotrit na Vovku:
Net, ne voidet tselikom on v dukhovku!
Papa v kladovke ishchet pilu,
Ochen' nuzhna buzhenina k stolu.

THE BOILING POT

A little boy fell into a boiling pot.
He screamed loudly, but quickly boiled.
For a long time dad and grandpa complained:
Dinner was completely ruined!

Маленький мальчик в кастрюлю свалился.
Громко кричал, но скоро сварился.
Долго ворчали папа и дед:
Полностью был испорчен обед!

Malen'kii mal'chik v kastriuliu svalilsia.
Gromko krichal, no skoro svarilsia.
Dolgo vorchali papa i ded:
Polnost'iu byl isporchen obed!

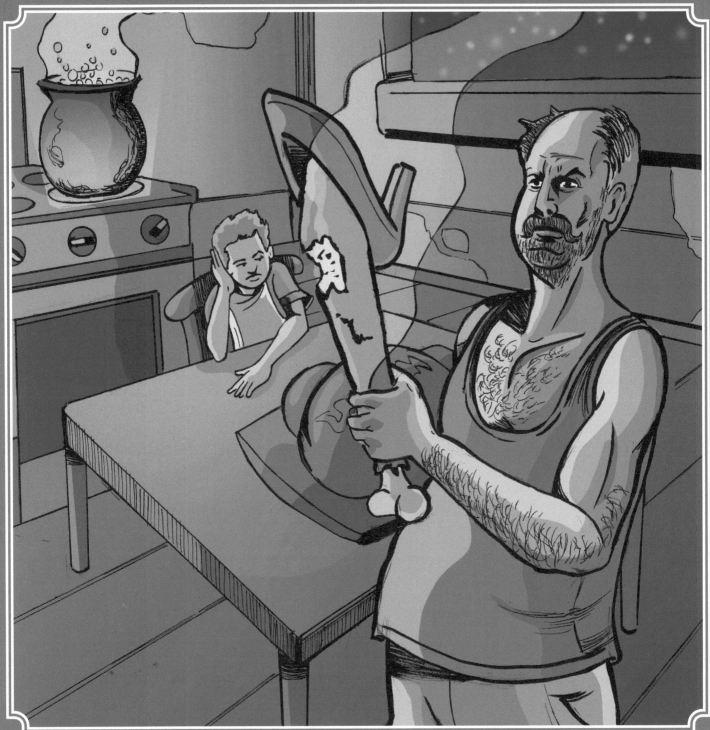

RUSSIAN OPTIMISM

GAMEY MEAT

Dad chewed meat in the kitchen.
"This is really gamey," he said.
Little Peter lowered his eyes in embarrassment.
"I boiled Aunt Fannie for a really long time!"

Папа на кухне мясо жевал.
" Жесткое очень ! " - он сыну сказал.
Петя смущенно глаза опустил:
"Я тетю Фросю долго варил !"

Papa na kukhne miaso zheval.
"Zhestkoe ochen'!"- on synu skazal.
Petia smushchenno glaza opustil:
"Ia tetiu Frosiu dolgo varil!"

RUSSIAN OPTIMISM

THE OVEN

A little boy found a grenade,
He hid it in the oven and went to school.
At night, grandma turned on the oven...
A lot of people came to her funeral.

Маленький мальчик гранату нашел,
В печку запрятал и в школу ушел.
Вечером бабушка печь растопила...
Много народу ее хоронило.

Malen'kii mal'chik granatu nashel,
V pechku zapriatal i v shkolu ushel.
Vecherom babushka pech' rastopila...
Mnogo narodu ee khoronilo.

RUSSIAN OPTIMISM

THE RAT

A little boy named Peter,
Found a rat and trapped it in the toilet.
In the morning dad walked in... Poor guy!
It's gonna be hard for him to live without testicles.

Маленький мальчик по имени Петя,
Крысу нашел и закрыл в туалете.
Утром зашел туда папа... Бедняжка!
Без яиц ему жить будет тяжко.

Malen'kii mal'chik po imeni Petia,
Krysu nashel i zakryl v tualete.
Utrom zashel tuda papa... Bedniazhka!
Bez iaits emu zhit' budet tiazhko.

RUSSIAN OPTIMISM

GOOD TIMING

Little Billy was climbing down from a tree,
A branch broke under his foot.
But he didn't hit the ground with a thud:
The crocodile opened its mouth just in time.

Маленький Билл с баобаба спускался,
С треском сучок под ногою сломался.
Но не ударился маленький Билл:
Вовремя пасть приоткрыл крокодил.

Malen'kii Bill s baobaba spuskalsia,
S treskom suchok pod nogoiu slomalsia.
No ne udarilsia malen'kii Bill:
Vovremia past' priotkryl krokodil.

RUSSIAN OPTIMISM

A CYPRUS VACATION

In the sky, a big plane flies,
It's bringing a bunch of people to Cyprus.
In one suitcase, something is ticking,
It's unlikely the plane will be found in the ocean.

В небе летит большой самолет,
Кучу народу на Кипр везет.
Тикает что-то в одном чемодане,
Вряд ли найдут самолет в океане.

V nebe letit bol'shoi samolet,
Kuchu narodu na Kipr vezet.
Tikaet chto-to v odnom chemodane,
Vriad li naidut samolet v okeane.

RUSSIAN OPTIMISM

THE FLOWER POT

Little Corey fell from the windowsill.
When he hit the ground, he stopped screaming.
Grandma quickly came into his room…
Whew! He didn't knock over the flower pot.

Маленький Костя с карниза сорвался,
Крик его вскоре внизу оборвался.
Бабушка в комнату кинулась ланью…
Нет! Не задел он горшочек с геранью.

Malen'kii Kostya s karniza sorvalsia,
Krik ego vskore vnizu oborvalsia.
Babushka v komnatu kinulas' lan'iu…
Net! Ne zadel on gorshochek s geran'iu.

RUSSIAN OPTIMISM

FATHER AND SON

A dad brought his son hunting.
He loaded his rifle with hollow point bullets.
He shot at the wolf, but hit his son.
"What a tragedy, I wasted a bullet!"

Отец на охоту сынка прихватил.
Жаканом ружьишко свое зарядил.
Выстрелил в волка - в сына попал.
"Вот ведь обида - патрон зря пропал!"

Otets na okhotu synka prikhvatil.
Zhakanom ruzh'ishko svoe zariadil.
Vystrelil v volka - v syna popal.
"Vot ved' obida - patron zria propal!"

RUSSIAN OPTIMISM

THE LOVELY COUPLE

A madly in-love couple strolled on the railroad tracks,
They chatted pleasantly and filled with desire.
Like an arrow, the Siberian express came through:
There used to be two people, now there are four.

Влюбленная пара по рельсам гуляла,
Мило болтала и томно вздыхала.
Стрелою пронесся экспресс из Сибири:
Было их двое, а стало четыре.

Vliublennaia para po rel'sam guliala,
Milo boltala i tomno vzdykhala.
Streloiu pronessia ekspress iz Sibiri:
Bylo ikh dvoe, a stalo chetyre.

RUSSIAN OPTIMISM

SURPRISE

A girl walked along with her crippled grandpa,
A gang of rapists caught up to them...
The gang was really surprised, that instead of a bad leg
Grandpa had an iron pipe!

Девочка с хроменьким дедушкой шла,
Банда насильников их догнала...
Кто мог подумать, что вместо ноги
У деда обрезок чугунной трубы!

Devoshka s khromen'kim dedushkoi shla,
Banda nasil'nikov ikh dognala...
Kto mog podumat', chto vmesto nogi
U deda obrezok chugunnoi truby!

44

THE HAPPY SINGERS

The children happily attend kindergarten,
The children happily sing.
Outside on the tree, carefully hang
A few children who poorly sang.

Весело дети в детсаде живут,
Весело дети песни поют.
А на ветвях развешаны в ряд
Несколько плохо поющих ребят.

Veselo deti v detsade zhivut,
Veselo deti pesni poiut.
A na vetviakh razveshany v riad
Neskol'ko plokho poiushchikh rebiat.

RUSSIAN OPTIMISM

THE ACTOR

Little Andrew turned on the vacuum cleaner,
He stuck his short nose inside.
Now without any makeup,
He can play Pinocchio in his school's play.

Мальчик Андрюша включил пылесос,
Сунул в него свой коротенький нос.
Может теперь он без помощи грима
В школьном театре играть Буратино.

Mal'chik Andriusha vkliuchil pylesos,
Sunul v nego svoi koroten'kii nos.
Mozhet teper' on bez pomoshchi grima
V shkol'nom teatre igrat' Buratino.

RUSSIAN OPTIMISM

THE ZAMBONI

Uncle Kirril knocked on the door:
"Your daughter was run over by a Zamboni," he said.
Mom asked anxiously, "How is she now?"
He replied, "Hold on, I'll slide her under the door!"

В дверь дома стучит дядя Кирилл:
- Вашу дочку ледовый каток задавил.
Мама воскликнула: - Что с ней теперь?
- Сейчас я ее вам просуну под дверь!

V dver' doma stuchit diadia Kirill.
- Vashu dochku ledoviy katok zadavil.
Mama voskliknula: - Chto s nei teper'?
- Seichas ia eyo Vam prosunu pod dver'!

RUSSIAN OPTIMISM

THE SANDBOX

A little boy played in a sandbox,
Quietly a cement truck snuck up on him.
You didn't hear a scream or a gasp,
Just his booties sticking out of the cement.

Маленький мальчик в песочке играл,
Тихо подъехал к нему самосвал.
Не было слышно ни крика, ни стона,
Только ботинки торчат из бетона.

Malen'kii mal'chik v pesochke igral,
Tikho pod'ekhal k nemu samosval.
Ne bylo slyshno ni krika, ni stona,
Tol'ko botinki torchat iz betona.

RUSSIAN OPTIMISM

ШIИDУ DАУ

A little boy inflated a large balloon,
A gust of strong wind blew,
A man watched the boy disappear but didn't rush over,
No one has seen the boy since.

Маленький мальчик шарик надул,
Сильный порывистый ветер подул,
Дядя глядел ему вслед не спеша,
Больше не видел никто малыша.

Malen'kii mal'chik sharik nadul,
Sil'nyi poryvistyi veter podul,
Diadia gliadel emu vsled ne spesha,
Bol'she ne videl nikto malysha.

RUSSIAN OPTIMISM

THE WOODS

A little boy found a machine gun
Nothing lives in the woods anymore.

Маленький мальчик нашёл пулемёт...
Больше в лесу никто не живёт.

Malen'kii mal'chik nashel pulemet...
Bol'she v lesu nikto ne zhivet.

RUSSIAN OPTIMISM

THE PINEAPPLE

Grandpa found a pineapple in the field,
He didn't think that it was a hand grenade.
He pulled out a knife and got ready to eat,
They found his ass six kilometers away.

Дедушка в поле нашел ананас,
Он не подумал, что это фугас.
Ножик достал он, собрался поесть,
Жопу нашли километров за шесть.

Dedushka v pole nashel ananas,
On ne podumal, chto eto fugas.
Nozhik dostal on, sobralsia poest',
Zhopu nashli kilometrov za shest'.

RUSSIAN OPTIMISM

THE SNORER

A daughter really loved her dad,
She turned on the gas stove.
Dad slept in the adjacent room,
He used to snore, now he stopped.

Девочка папочку очень любила,
Краник у газовой плитки открыла.
Папа в соседней комнате спал,
Раньше храпел, а теперь перестал.

Devochka papochku ochen' liubila,
Kranik u gazovoi plitki otkryla.
Papa v sosednei komnate spal,
Ran'she khrapel, a teper' perestal.

RUSSIAN OPTIMISM

THIS LAST ONE MAKES NO SENSE

A little boy quietly played in the kitchen.
A bulldozer came up from behind.
"A bulldozer in the kitchen? Haha! That's bullshit!"
You're laughing? Okay, laugh. But the boy is dead.

Мальчик на кухне тихонько играл.
Сзади бульдозер к нему подъезжал.
"Бульдозер на кухне? Ха-ха! Это бред!"
Смеётесь? Ну, смейтесь. А мальчика нет.

Mal'chik na kukhne tikhon'ko igral.
Szadi bul'dozer k nemu pod'ezzhal.
"Bul'dozer na kukhne? Kha-kha! Eto bred!"
Smeetes'? Nu, smeites'. A mal'chika net.

RUSSIAN OPTIMISM

ABOUT THE CREATORS

Ben Rosenfeld is a New York City based stand-up comedian and writer who has appeared on FOX's *Laughs*, *CBS This Morning* and Rooftop Comedy. He was featured as TimeOut New York's Joke of the Week and has headlined at Caroline's on Broadway. He is

the co-host of the weekly podcast, *The Passive Aggressive Podcast* and has a comedy album, *Neuro Comedy*, both of which are available on iTunes.

Ben was born in the Soviet Union and his family immigrated to America when he was a child. Before becoming a full-time comedian, he worked as a management consultant for Accenture, a Fortune 500 technology company, and was enrolled in a neuro economics Ph.D. program at Caltech on a full scholarship.

Ben previously wrote *How To Find Your Passion*, an e-book and motivational seminar that helps high school and college students more closely define their future career choices.

See More Of Ben At: **BigBenComedy.com**

Dov Smiley is a published comic artist and illustrator. Having studied at both the Ontario College of Art and Design (OCAD) and the Kubert School, Dov's body

of work can be found in various publications and anthologies. Most recently, Dov self-published *The Book of Jonah*, which can be found on his website: **JonahComic.com**.

Dov is not Russian...and is really hoping Russians have a good sense of humor.

Chris James is a print designer. He sees the world in Cyan, Magenta, Yellow, and Black. He's an art school graduate who is consumed with regrets about attending art

school. He's also a stand-up comedian and speaker. His one man show, *Half-Lesbian - A Straight Dude's Guide to Growing Up With Lesbian Parents*, has earned him praise.

More about Chris can be found on his site: **RaisedUnderPowerLines.com**.

See Bonus Material and Order More Copies Of The Book At: **www.RussianOptimism.com**

CPSIA information can be obtained
at www.ICGtesting.com
Printed in the USA
BVHW091254010921
615792BV00001B/1